When Grubby hears a strange noise one winter's day, he thinks it is a giant Snowzo. "Snowzos don't exist," scoffed Newton Gimmick. But even Gimmick is convinced that Snowzos do exist when he comes face to face with the giant creature from the woods.

British Library Cataloguing in Publication Data

Miller, Dennis
   A surprise visitor.
   I. Title
   823'.914[J]
   ISBN 0-7214-1169-X

Designed by R W Ditchfield

First edition

Published by Ladybird Books Ltd Loughborough Leicestershire UK
Ladybird Books Inc Auburn Maine 04210 USA

Printed in England

A surprise visitor

adapted by DENNIS MILLER

Ladybird Books

One very cold and snowy day
the Wooly What's-It invited
Teddy Ruxpin and Newton
Gimmick to supper. Grubby and
Fuzz the Fob were going, too.

Wooly went out to
meet them as the
Airship came in to
land. But when they
jumped down, they
found themselves
chin-deep in a
snowdrift!

"Good of you to drop in!" joked Wooly as he scooped them up and carried them to his house.

Suddenly, an eerie cry of *Br-br-br-br-wha-ha-ha!* came echoing on the wind.

"What's that noise?" asked Teddy nervously.

"It's only the wind!" Gimmick explained.

"Then it was a very big wind!" answered Grubby. And Fuzz the Fob added, "Very big indeed!"

Wooly led the others indoors, where it was warm and cosy.

Grubby was still outside on the

doorstep taking
off the last of his
six snowboots.
Once again, the
same eerie
sound came
echoing across
the snow —
*Br-br-br-br-
wha-ha-ha!*

Grubby came crashing in through the door with his arms and legs in a terrible tangle. As he fell flat on his face he cried, "Did you hear that? There's something outside and it sounds awfully big!"

"There's nothing out there," said Gimmick. "People often think they can see strange things during winter storms. Some people even imagine they can see giant Snowzos!"

"What do Snowzos look like?" squeaked Fuzz.

"Nothing," replied Gimmick, "because they don't exist!"

But Teddy and his friends didn't seem too sure. They were all thinking about that strange cry, *Br-br-br-br-wha-ha-ha!*

Wooly cooked them all a delicious supper. Everyone enjoyed it so much that they soon forgot about Snowzos until there was a loud knock at the door. Everyone except Gimmick dived for cover! But it was only three cold and very frightened Fobs. "We heard a Snowzo in the forest," they cried.

But Gimmick said again, "There are no such things as Snowzos!" Yet when there was another loud knocking at the door they all took cover — just in case Gimmick was wrong!

They waited anxiously to see who was there.

It was Gramps and Wiggs Woggley. They were frightened because they'd seen a Snowzo in the forest.

"It was big and furry," said Gramps. "It looked like a giant snowman with a beard!"

"Nonsense," said Gimmick. "It was probably just a pile of snow. Besides, Wooly is big and strong. He would protect us from Snowzos — if there were such creatures."

But Wooly was hiding under  the table! Grubby, the Fobs, Teddy and the Wogglies soon joined him there.

Everyone began to feel much more cheerful when Wooly brought them mugs of hot grundleberry juice to drink in front of the fire. But when they ran out of firewood, no one wanted to go outside and fetch some more.

At last Teddy and Wooly offered to get the logs.

In the garden, a cold wind whipped the snow into whirls and swirls. Teddy and Wooly couldn't see where they were going. They didn't realise that they were on different paths. Nor did they realise that something large and white with floppy hair was following Teddy.

When Teddy reached the woodpile the white furry creature came to a halt behind him. Teddy thought that the creature was Wooly, covered in snow from head to toe.

In no time at all they had collected a big pile of logs and marched back towards the house.

Teddy thought that Wooly was joking when he heard him call, "Have you found the woodpile yet, Teddy?"

Gimmick, Grubby, the Fobs and the Wogglies were all delighted to see Teddy and the large white creature.

"Oh Wooly," cried Grubby, "you're all covered in snow!" But when he tried to brush away the snow, it wouldn't come off!

Just then, the door opened and in walked the real Wooly. Everyone looked at Wooly. Then they looked at the giant creature with the floppy hair. Gimmick gulped. "Er, if this creature isn't Wooly, then he must be…"

"…A Snowzo!" yelped the others as they dived for cover.

But the Snowzo was friendly! He explained that Snowzos usually lived far away in the northern Land of Ying, and only came south during very cold and snowy winters.

"Your voice is just like Wooly's!" said Teddy. "You even look like Wooly, except that he's purple and you're white."

The Snowzo gazed at Wooly and said, "We have a legend about a young Snowzo who wandered away from the mountain and was never seen again. Wooly might be that Snowzo!"

Teddy and his friends gasped. Was Wooly a Snowzo?

Indeed, Wooly had never been sure where he had come from, and Gimmick had always said that Wooly got his purple colour from bathing in Rainbow Falls. So Wooly might well be the Snowzo's long-lost cousin! He was thrilled at the idea of having a family.

"Excuse me!"
Teddy said to the
Snowzo. "You said,
We have a legend…
Are there lots of Snowzos?"

"There certainly
are!" answered
the Snowzo. He
moved over to
the door and
threw it open.

"Br-br-br-br-wha-ha-ha!" he cried.

One by one, Snowzos began
popping up all over the garden.
Some were young, some were old,
but all were white with floppy hair
and they all looked like Wooly!

Teddy and his friends went out into
the garden to meet them.

The Snowzos were amazed when they saw Wooly! "Just fancy!" they kept exclaiming. "A purple Snowzo! Whoever would have thought of such a thing?"

Wooly wanted to know all about the Land of Ying and promised to visit his long-lost cousins as soon as the weather got warmer.

All too soon it was time for the Snowzos to return home. Teddy and his friends watched them disappear northwards towards the mountains.

"Well!" said Grubby, as they turned back to the house. "I've learned something new today!"

"What's that, Grubby?" asked Teddy.

"I know why Snowzos say *Br-br-br-br-wha-ha-ha!*" replied Grubby.

"All right! Why do they say *Br-br-br-br-wha-ha-ha?*" said Teddy.

"It's just their way of saying, *I'm so co-ooo-old!*" And laughing happily, the friends went back inside Wooly's cosy house. Never again would any of them be afraid of the Snowzos!